HANDY-DANDY
HELPFUL HAL
A BOOK ABOUT
HELPFULNESS

Michael P. Waite
Illustrated by Gary Trousdale

Chariot Books
DAVID C. COOK PUBLISHING CO.

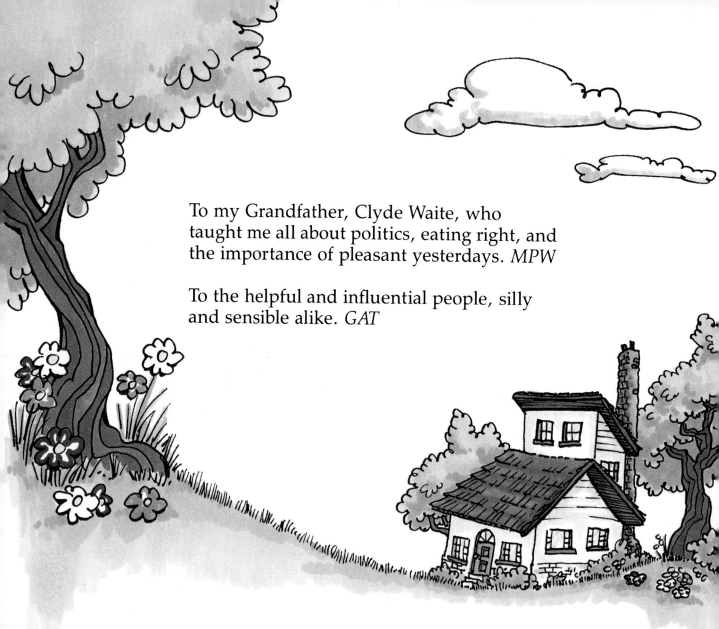

To my Grandfather, Clyde Waite, who taught me all about politics, eating right, and the importance of pleasant yesterdays. *MPW*

To the helpful and influential people, silly and sensible alike. *GAT*

Chariot Books is an imprint of David C. Cook Publishing Co.
David C. Cook Publishing Co., Elgin, Illinois 60120
David C. Cook Publishing Co., Weston, Ontario

HANDY-DANDY HELPFUL HAL
© 1987 by Michael P. Waite for text and illustrations

Cover design by Dawn Lauck
First printing, 1987
Printed in the United States of America
92 91 90   5 4

Library of Congress Cataloging-in-Publication Data
Waite, Michael P., 1960-
    Handy-Dandy Helpful Hal.
    (Building Christian character series)
    Summary: Helpful Hal shows Sam and Sue the importance of helping their parents by doing chores such as hanging up clothes, washing the car, and feeding the cat.
    [1. Helpfulness—Fiction. 2. Family life—Fiction. 3. Christian life—Fiction. 4. Stories in rhyme] I. Trousdale, Gary, ill. II. Title. III. Series: Waite, Michael P., 1960-   . Building Christian character series.
PZ8.3.W136Han 1987   [E]   87-5275
ISBN 1-55513-221-9

Dear Mom and Dad,

Did you ever hide your child's pill in a spoonful of jelly? That's how the lesson about helpfulness is tucked into *Handy-Dandy Helpful Hal*. The teaching is couched in a fun, rhyming story.

You and your children can't help but smile at Hal and his painless approach to helping with household chores. But there's no missing his message: Kids need to learn to be helpful.

How can you use this book to help train your children?

Read *Handy-Dandy Helpful Hal* aloud, as a family. Talk about the story and why being helpful is important for God's children. Discuss Colossians 3:23, the verse found on page 31, and memorize it together. The verse will serve as a reminder of the Christian character trait of helpfulness.

Use catch words from the story to remind each other of the lesson: "I need a 'Pooped-Out Parent's Perfect Pal' " may become your family's code for "please help me with these chores."

Young readers will enjoy reading the book to themselves and to their younger brothers and sisters. Nonreaders can tell themselves the story by looking at the pictures after it's been read aloud a couple of times.

Building Christian character is hard work—but it can be done in an enjoyable way, as *Handy-Dandy Helpful Hal* points out.

There we were, in our backyard,
My wife and I were working hard.
We had a giant list of chores . . .
To be exact, nine-thousand-four!

Both our children, Sam and Sue,
Told us they had things to do . . .
Like sipping slushy lemonade
On the hammock, in the shade!

As I wiped my sweaty brow,
And rested on my rusty plow,
A funny fellow came my way.
He crossed my lawn and said, "Good day!"

He pulled a wagon full of things—
Like tools and mops and paints and strings.
That man had gadgets everywhere—
Inside his boots, up to his hair!

He came right up and shook my hand,
"Aha!" he said, "You're just the man!
I'm Handy-Dandy Helpful Hal,
The Pooped-Out Parents' Perfect Pal!"

Hal went up to Sam and Sue
And whispered in their ears, "Yoooo Hoooo!
Up and at 'em, sleepy heads,
Mom and Pop are pooped," he said.
"Time for you to lend a hand,
Better help them while you can!"

"With all this lying 'round like slugs
I'm sure you'll both turn into Gluggs.
I'm sure you've heard of Gluggs before?
All they do is eat and snore—
Giant things, all green and chubby. . . .
Say there, Sam, you're getting tubby."

Next thing I knew my feet were draggin'
Off the back of Hal's big wagon. . . .

Through the door with one quick pounce,
And up the stairs without a bounce.

13

He rolled us into Sammy's room
And handed Sam a purple broom.
"Time to clean your room," he said,
"Do you know how to make a bed?
These are chores a kid can do. . . .
I've cleaned my room since I was two."

My wife and I were quite surprised—
The kids cleaned up before our eyes!

No sooner had they finished that
Than Hal called in the dog and cat.

"I think these pets are yours," he said.
"Every day they must be fed.
A simple chore, I think you'll find,
Let's try it once, if you don't mind!"

16

Sam and Sue each filled a dish
With Puppy Pork and Frisky Fish.
They filled the other bowls with water.
Could this be MY son and daughter?

"Good!" said Hal and off we went
Like a hound dog on a scent.
At the kitchen sink he stopped
And said, "I'll need you, Mom and Pop!"

"These kids can wash the pots and pans,
But they have tiny little hands,
And so it's best if everyone
Joins in to get the dishes done!"

19

Before we knew what Hal was saying
Soap was sudsing, water spraying.
Soon we had those dishes clean—
Washed and dried just like a dream!

"While we're here," said Helpful Hal,
"Shall we do more? I think we shall!
Here we have the kitchen trash,
You can dump it in a flash!
Just put it in a plastic bag,
And out you go . . . don't let it drag!"

"Very nicely done!" said Hal.
"I told you I'm a parents' pal!
Now off we go! Out to the yard!
I'll bet these kids can wash a car!"

"Here's a chore we all can do,"
Said Hal, and then the water flew.
"I've washed at least a million cars,
I've washed the cars of Movie Stars!
And if, perhaps, you think I'm fibbin'
Here's my First—Place Washer's Ribbon!"

23

Susie hosed while Sammy scrubbed,
We soaped and washed and wiped and rubbed,

And soon that car was shiny bright.
"Good job!" said Hal. "You've done all right."

"Now quickly, let's complete our chores,
We'll pull some weeds since we're outdoors—
Be sure you check with Mom or Pop
So you don't yank a carrot top!"

"Last of all, let's get the rake
And pile these leaves, for goodness sake!
And when we've made a giant heap,
It's lots of fun to take a leap!"

"There!" said Hal. "I think we're done!
Wasn't that a lot of fun?
You were splendid, Sam and Sue—
See the things that you can do?"

"When you help your mom and dad
The chores don't really seem so bad.
And everything gets done so soon,
That you still have the afternoon!"

"Why not travel to the ocean?
Don't forget your suntan lotion!
How about a camping trip?
Go to the pool and take a dip!
A game of tennis? Maybe two?
When did you last see the zoo?"

28

"Thank you, Helpful Hal," I said.
"You've taught our kids to make their beds,
You showed them how to feed the cat,
And how to wash the car in fact!
You showed them how to fold their clothes,
And on and on your helping goes."

"But now that we have done our chores,
There's something else to do outdoors—
Swimming, zoos, and mountain hikes
Aren't the sort of things we like.
I hope that you won't think us rude,
But we have quite another mood!"

And with those words, my wife and I
Took our children at our side
And crawled up on the hammock swing
To do our very favorite thing!

Whatever you do, work at it with all your heart, as working for the Lord, not for men.

Colossians 3:23 (NIV)

Look for all the great stories in the
Building Christian Character series

Buzzle Billy—A Book About Sharing
Handy-Dandy Helpful Hal—A Book About Helpfulness
Miggy and Tiggy—A Book About Overcoming Jealousy
Suzy Swoof—A Book About Kindness
Max and the Big Fat Lie—A Book About Telling the Truth
Casey the Greedy Young Cowboy—A Book About Being Thankful
Sir Maggie the Mighty—A Book About Obedience
Boggin, Blizzy, and Sleeter the Cheater—A Book About Fairness